This Ainu tale was written by Hisakazu Fujimura, as told to him by Yae Shitaku, a descendent of the Ainu people of Japan. The translation was made by Cathy Hirano.

HO-LIMLIM

A RABBIT TALE FROM JAPAN

by TEJIMA

PHILOMEL BOOKS   NEW YORK

Ho-limlim, ho-limlim.
Once I leapt and bounded,
flying over hill and field, through
river and wood, going wherever my fancy took me.

In the spring, I feasted on the tender shoots
of trees and grasses, and in the autumn, I filled my belly
with ripe fruits and berries.
Ho-limlim, ho-limlim.

But that was a long time ago.

Now, I have grown so old I spend most of my days
basking in the sun where the snow has melted,
my head nodding as I doze.

But one day, the cold morning air woke me.
When I went outside, the sun had just raised its head
above a high snow-capped mountain. I could smell
spring in the wind. I decided to venture out.

When I saw the blue of the ocean from the top
of a hill, I started down to the shore.
Ho-limlim, ho-limlim.
Through two little brooks, over three streams.
Ho-limim, ho-limlim.

Through two woods and three meadows.
Ho-limlim, ho-limlim.
My feet kicked the ground lightly, and the wind
rushed in my ears.

From the top of a dune I looked across the bay.
The blue sea spread out as far as I could see.
Waves rolled lazily toward the shore, and sea spray
foamed and hissed as the waves hit the sand.
Boom, boom. Shhhh.
Boom, boom. Shhhh.

Suddenly, on the horizon, I saw a whale
as big as a small hill lying on the beach.
Squinting to get a better look, I saw men dressed
in white and black busily carrying away the

blubber and meat. "I will help," I thought.
"If I am lucky, they might give me some and
I will dine on whale stew tonight. Mmmm. I must
hurry." So I ran and ran.
Ho-limlim, ho-limlim.

But when I came to the place, the huge whale
was just seaweed and old wood tossed up on the
shore by the sea. The busy men were just black crows
and white gulls! I decided I might as well go home.

I took the long way home around the forest.
Although there was still snow under the trees,
juicy-looking shoots were sprouting up. They
might be ready to eat in two or three days.

Then I ran along the bank. I saw two people fighting and splashing each other in the middle of the river. "I must put a stop to that," I thought. I leapt into the river and ran through the icy water toward them.

But the fighting men I had thought to stop
were nothing but a fish trap. Its wooden posts,
loosened by ice and water, were
waving wildly in the stream.

"What am I seeing?" I asked myself. The
melting snow chilled my skin and drops of water
ran from my fur. Pop, pop. Pop, pop.
With heavy steps I set off toward home again.

As I approached the forest where I lived,
my heart almost stopped beating.

Thick black smoke rose into the air above
my home. Fire! I ran and ran to see what
I could save.

My breath came in gasps, puff, puff, and my heart
felt as though it would burst. But when I reached
my home, it was just as I had left it! The smoke
was only a thundercloud rising up from the mountain behind.

From that time to this, my children and grandchildren
bring me good things to eat. They listen happily
to the tales of my youth. On a nice day, I nap in the sun.

And that is how I enjoy life, ho-limlim, ho-limlim,
because when you get old, and your eyes play tricks,
ho-limlim, ho-limlim,
venturing out is good but home is even better.

That is how one Isopo Kamuy, an old rabbit god, told
the tale to man.

About HO-LIMLIM

HO-LIMLIM takes place in Hokkaido, the northernmost island of Japan and home of the Ainu people, a disappearing race thought to be the country's original inhabitants. It is one of many ancient tales of the Ainu. Their tales (called *Yukara*) are sung, and each individual *Yukara* has its own musical effect. Only recently have these fascinating musical stories of Ainu gods, legends, and mysteries been written down. This original story of an aging rabbit was collected by Hisakazu Fujimura, as told to him by an old Ainu woman.

The rabbit, to the Ainu people, is an extremely important animal. Not only is it a vital part of their diet, but the rabbit was originally believed to have curative powers and protective charms. If people did not show due respect and appreciation, this gentle god became quite fearsome. Accordingly, the rabbit is respectfully referred to as *isopo kamuy* (rabbit-god). The repetitive phrase *ho-limlim, ho-limlim* evokes the image of the rabbit god bounding lightly over the fields.

Originally published in Japan in 1988 under the title *Isopo Kamuy* by Fukutake Publishing Co., Ltd., Tokyo, Japan. Illustrations copyright © 1988 Keizaburō Tejima. Text copyright © 1988 Hisakazu Fujimura. Based on an English translation by Cathy Hirano arranged through Fukutake Publishing Co., Ltd. English-language translation copyright © 1990 by Philomel Books. Published in the United States by Philomel Books, a division of The Putnam & Grosset Book Group, 200 Madison Avenue, New York, NY 10016. Published simultaneously in Canada. All rights reserved. Printed in Japan. Book design by Christy Hale.

Library of Congress Cataloging-in-Publication Data. Tejima, Keizaburō. [Isopo kamuy. English] Ho-limlim/A Rabbit Story/by Keizaburō Tejima. p. cm. Summary: After one last foray far from his home, an aging rabbit decides he prefers to rest in his own garden and let his children and grandchildren bring him good things to eat. [1. Old age—Fiction. 2. Rabbits—Fiction.] I. Title. PZ7.T234Rab 1990 89-26596 CIP AC [E]—dc20 ISBN 0-399-22156-5

First Impression